William Hunt

An Address upon the Late Joseph Leidy

his university career

William Hunt

An Address upon the Late Joseph Leidy
his university career

ISBN/EAN: 9783337426842

Printed in Europe, USA, Canada, Australia, Japan

Cover: Foto ©Andreas Hilbeck / pixelio.de

More available books at **www.hansebooks.com**

AN ADDRESS

UPON THE LATE

JOSEPH LEIDY, M.D., LL.D.,

HIS UNIVERSITY CAREER.

BY

WILLIAM HUNT, M.D.

Delivered November 17th, 1891,

BEFORE THE

ALUMNI AND STUDENTS OF THE MEDICAL DEPARTMENT
OF THE UNIVERSITY OF PENNSYLVANIA.

PHILADELPHIA:
COLLINS PRINTING HOUSE, 705 JAYNE STREET,
1892.

Dr. Alfred Stillé, in introducing the speaker, said :—

Gentlemen : Medical Alumni and Students of the University of Pennsylvania :—

We are assembled to listen to an address in commemoration of the late Professor of Anatomy in the University. You will recall the shock that was felt throughout the whole medical profession on the announcement that Dr. Leidy was dead.

It is most fitting that here in the centre of the University where he passed so many years of his active and laborious, and yet serene and unselfish life, and in the presence of those whom he enlightened and stimulated, his career should be described by one who was familiar with his character and labors, and is competent to portray them.

No doubt he will tell you that Leidy, though dead, still speaks to you. His living voice, indeed, is silent forever, but the memory of the great works he wrought in natural science, and the thoroughness and impressiveness of his teaching, must long survive to stimulate sincere searchers after truth, and to prove anew that the most consummate attainments in science are in perfect harmony with humility of character and simplicity of life.

Permit me to ask your attention to the address now to be delivered by Dr. William Hunt.

(5)

AN ADDRESS.

When first I was asked to speak before the alumni about Dr. Leidy I declined, because I had already spoken of his personal history at that remarkable meeting held at the Academy of Natural Sciences upon the evening of the 12th of May, 1891, only thirteen days after his death. I say remarkable meeting, for it was one of true emotion. Science was subdued in sorrow. The hall was filled with people of both sexes ready to mingle their tears in mutual sympathy at the realization of the fact that each and all had sustained an irreparable loss.

It was as much as we seven could do to get safely through our allotted tasks, and the others who spoke were equally affected. The programme named the following seven, and from fifteen to twenty-five minutes were occupied by each one :—

WILLIAM HUNT, M.D., "Personal History."

HARRISON ALLEN, M.D., "Work in Vertebrate Anatomy."

HENRY C. CHAPMAN, M.D., "Work in Invertebrate Anatomy."

Prof. ANGELO HEILPRIN, "Work in Paleontology and Geology."

JOSEPH WILLCOX, "Work in Mineralogy."

JAMES DARRACH, M.D., "Work in Botany."

EDWARD J. NOLAN, M.D., "Personal Character and Services to the Academy."

Here are six branches of science mentioned in this catalogue concerning which, if an ordinary man of science makes a name in one of them, he and others consider his life well spent, and yet Dr. Leidy was an expert and authority in all.

Now, this is what made me, on second thought, accept the invitation to appear before you to-night. A small edition of my remarks was printed for private circulation. In it I use the above unique programme for a preface, for nothing more was required, and in it I also fortunately say, "The personal history of Dr. Leidy is all that has been assigned to me to talk about for these few minutes, and, therefore, I leave to others the task of speaking of his University scientific career." That career, however, was not sufficiently spoken of, so pressing were other matters, and thus I have my opportunity. The University career and other allied matters that may occur to me in my intimate association with Dr. Leidy, will, therefore, occupy us this evening.

But, before going on, there is one to whom full thanks must be given for setting forth Dr. Leidy's work in his University professorship, as well as his other vast work in science.

This was not done on the evening referred to, but the Academy, whilst retaining in its possession the almost impromptu essays of the evening, concluded, by resolution, not to publish them, but to have prepared a more complete memoir for publication in its proceedings. This task was assigned to Professor Henry C. Chapman, now of the Jefferson Medical College, but who was for a long time connected with this University, from which he is a graduate as his grandfather was, and chiefly in association with his beloved friend, Dr. Joseph Leidy. In the last number of the Proceedings of the Academy of Natural Sciences this more completed memoir appears. Right well has the task been done, and great labor was expended in the doing of it. At the conclusion the writer says: "The following catalogue of volumes, papers, and communications, published by Dr. Joseph Leidy, illustrates the extent, variety, and value of his contributions to science. " And then follows a bibliography containing the titles of, and references to, *five hundred and fifty-three* of these books, papers, and essays, published from the time just as he had reached manhood, almost unto the day of his death. Think of this, you men, who have groaned at *one* graduating essay! There is another thing to reflect upon. I take it, that possibly with the exception of some little pay for his early translations and pay for his Treatise on Human Anatomy, all or nearly all of this vast literary, critical, searching, scientific work was done without pecuniary fee or reward. It may be that is the reason most of you do not like that kind of work, and my jibe is unjust. I am sure I have often said to myself, after toiling for days and nights at some paper of scientific or literary research and interest, and then getting a petty check for it, or, what is more common, nothing at all, " What fools we mortals be." To be sure, we do not do our *great work* for money, but the " *Res angusta domi*" are always calling for bread from somewhere.

Dr. Leidy was born on September 9th, 1823,

and died on April 30th, 1891, in the 68th year of his age. He was of German extraction, the son of Philip Leidy, a hatter, of North Third Street, Philadelphia, and Catharine, his wife. The mother died while he was yet a baby. The father married Christiana Mellick, a sister of his first wife. She proved to be a most loving and faithful mother to her stepson, and he often said that he owed all he was to her.

How he began very early to notice natural objects of every kind, to roam in the fields and the woods, and upon the streams is fully noticed in the sketches of him already published.

For this occasion we will take up his life when he began to study medicine. He did not do this without opposition from his father, although his mother favored the project.

Finally the boy and the mother won. In those days all students of medicine had to have a preceptor in name, if not in fact. Leidy entered the office of Dr. James McClintock, a noted lecturer on anatomy. He did not remain in that office throughout his pupilage, but for some reason left it and entered with Dr. Paul B. Goddard, a most noted anatomist, author, and teacher, a Lecturer and Demonstrator of Anatomy in this University ;

a genius, well trained by nature and opportunity in the use of his perceptive qualities, and withal very congenial and instructive to a young man having the receptive temperament of Dr. Leidy.

Dr. Leidy graduated in 1844. His thesis showed his tendencies. It was upon "The Comparative Anatomy of the Eye of Vertebrated Animals."

He became prosector at the University for Professor Horner, who filled the Anatomical Chair. For *one* year (1846) he left the University to take the place of Demonstrator of Anatomy in the Franklin Medical College, a new institution in which Dr. Paul B. Goddard, his former preceptor, whom he thought it was his duty to follow, was Professor of Anatomy. The school had but a short life, and the doctor soon returned to his former place with Dr. Horner. With this exception he never broke his allegiance to the University from his graduation until his death. He had several great temptations, notably one of a professorship in Harvard, but, after much consideration, he chose to stand by his old colors.

It was at this time (1846) that I began the study of medicine with the late Dr. George B. Wood, then in his prime, as my preceptor. Had it not been for such a man as he was, together with the introduction of some young blood, as in the case of John Neill, the energetic Lecturer and Demonstrator of Anatomy, and Joseph Leidy the prosector, I can assure you that the University Medical School at that time was in a state of "innocuous desuetude," or, if you choose, of medical dotage or senility. This is said with no disrespect, but simply as an illustration of the axiom, "that few die and none resign;" the school was living on the past; and with few exceptions we sought our information outside of, instead of within it. There were several corps of first-rate young teachers on the outskirts, most of whom rose to distinguished positions afterwards. Dr. Wood knew these well, and through his students patronized the practical branches without stint. This was almost a heresy, but the fact is that Dr. Wood at that early day was a pioneer in the present methods of teaching.

He was always practical and demonstrative, and being blessed with wealth he spared nothing to illustrate what was worth knowing. His materia medica lectures were illustrated with medical plants in profusion from his own green-houses, and when he became Professor of Practice in 1849,

Dr. Leidy went to Europe with him in order to assist him to make a pathological collection. We have what I may call the remnant of that collection in the museum of the University now. Dr. Leidy mounted and had charge of the early specimens, and after he became Professor of Anatomy, they fell under the charge of Dr. Levick and myself. When I go through the museum now I still recognize some of my old work. Understand, besides being kept up by importations from abroad during Dr. Wood's incumbency of the Chair of Practice, the collection was constantly enriched by contributions from home. Dr. Leidy, the year before, had gone to Europe with Dr. Horner. Young as he was, he had already won such a reputation in science that he was received everywhere with *éclat* by the most noted savants both old and young. Horner's lectures, now enriched by Leidy's magnificent dissections, and John Neill's practical recapitulations in the evening, made the study of anatomy a pleasure instead of a toil, and in that branch also we now got more from within the building than from without.

You must bear in mind that what I personally have knowledge of in my intimate association with Dr. Leidy mostly happened at the old building in Ninth Street, where the Post-office now stands. Owing to the failure of Professor Horner's health in 1852, Dr. Leidy was appointed by the trustees to finish the course of lectures for that year. In 1853 Professor Horner died, and Dr. Leidy, then only thirty years of age, was, after a sharp contest, elected Professor of Anatomy in the University of Pennsylvania. He appointed his old friend, Dr. Fitzwilliam Sargent, his Demonstrator of Anatomy, but he only served for one term. Dr. Sargent left Philadelphia and spent the rest of his days in Italy and Paris, now and then paying a visit to this country. He has recently died, but has left to the world a son, a most distinguished artist, John S. Sargent. Dr. Leidy in 1854 chose me for his successor. I filled the place as Demonstrator and Lecturer for ten years, and hence arose my close intimacy with our great professor, both as a sitter at the feet of Gamaliel in science, and as a companion and friend.

Untiring industry and systematic punctuality were the secrets of Dr. Leidy's life, and of its great results. I never even by chance dropped in upon him at his home, or in the University, and found him idle. He was always at work, and mostly at important work; but, whatever the work might be, he would stop and explain, or go on and explain, and having, as he thought at least, an appreciative listener, I always found myself learning something that I did not know before. There was never any pretence at mystery, or any seeking for seclusion. Are not these qualities, after all, among the real distinctions between genius and mediocrity?

My, my! think of the time most of us waste! Leidy took his holidays mindful of the old precept, "All work and no play," but his play even was but a variation of his home work, the sea, the mountains, and the woods being his playgrounds. Some of his most beautiful and interesting contributions to knowledge arose from these recreations.

Two rooms on the second floor of the old University, with a passage-way leading to the museum, the lecture, and dissecting-rooms, were the seat of Dr. Leidy's labors on Ninth Street. In a corner of the passage-way near the window were Fred. Schafhirt's tables, where he dissected and prepared reptiles, birds, and mammals, and ate schweitzer and drank schnaps, and sang German sentimental and patriotic songs. In the room adjoining was Leidy, may be dissecting a subject, and waited upon by the noiseless Johnny Brown, and the hinkende Mephistophelean Bob Nash.

Nothing could exceed the splendor of Leidy's dissections. Call to mind you who remember them, in his palmy days, the display of the diaphragm, the muscles of the abdomen and chest, and the wonders of the hand, the thoracic and abdominal viscera, and the clear and concise explanation and exhibitions of the human brain ! Leidy did very little in topographical anatomy (that he left to his demonstrators) so that what he displayed was the thing itself, whether it was bone, muscle, ligament, tendon, viscus, vessel, or nerve, and he spared nothing that came in the way of showing that thing. He was a fine free-hand draughtsman, and made much use of the blackboard to enforce his demonstrations.

I need but refer you to his work on the rhizopods to convince you that he was also an advanced artist in the delineation and coloring of microscopic objects than which, in the whole range of artistic procedures, there is nothing more difficult and absolutely requiring most special knowledge.

It was in these rooms (about 1858) that the fossil bones of the great lizard, the Hadrosaurus Foulkii, were studied and placed in position. They had recently been discovered in the marl near Woodbury, New Jersey, and were presented to the Academy of Natural Sciences by Wm. Parker Foulke, then one of its most active members. The studies of Dr. Leidy gave Mr. Waterhouse Hawkins an easy key for the restoration of the skeleton of the animal, which now forms such a conspicuous object in the collection of the Academy.

Some years before this, and before Dr. Leidy was professor (about 1846), he made his most important discovery, as far as regards the health and happiness of his fellow-beings, and also one at the present moment involving questions of the gravest import in international comity, and seriously attracting the attention of sovereigns, presidents, and ministers, millions of money being at stake in the results. I allude to the discovery of the trichina spiralis in the hog, the study of which the discoverer followed out in these rooms for years at every opportunity.

The trichina is a small nematoid worm about one-eighth of an inch long. Paget found it in human muscles in 1835, and Owen described and named it, but they, nor no one else knew or suspected from whence it came. Dr. Leidy, with characteristic modesty, in his description of it in Pepper's System of Medicine and calling himself "the writer," says, "In 1846 the parasite was found by the writer in the muscles of the hog, but neither he nor others for some time afterwards suspected the significance of the discovery." We now know that the immature trichina are swallowed by man whilst eating raw or underdone pork, the sick hog having most probably gotten them from devouring infected rats, and that the embryos undergo rapid development in the intestines, and actively migrate in myriads to the human muscles, thus giving rise to the painful, often fatal, disease, trichinosis. Dr. Leidy says a single ounce of the infected meat will often contain from 50,000 to 100,000 of the worms. (I was with and assisted Dr. Leidy once at the dissection of a man who had died of trichinosis.) He also says in his account, "The writer may also add that it was in a slice of boiled ham, from which he had partly made his dinner, that he first discovered trichina in the hog."

The simple preventive is : 1st, never to eat infected pork ; you may suspect it when you see very small white specks in the meat, these may be the trichina capsules ; and 2d, whether infected or not, never eat pork or any of its belongings unless it is thoroughly cooked, for a "boiling temperature surely kills all animal parasites." The same may be said of other meats infected with other parasites. Europeans, especially Germans, are much more inclined to eat raw, or half done, pork than we are. The great German helminthologists, Leuckart, Cobbold, and others have fully acknowledged the discovery as due to Dr. Leidy, and cheerfully accord him the credit of it.

Just as I had written this, I read from a morning paper the following, and I repeat it both for your information and consolation :—

Paris, Oct. 29, 1891.—The Senate to-day declared urgent the discussion on the question of duty on salt meats. Roche, Minister of Commerce, read a number of reports, showing that trichinosis did not exist in Great Britain and Belgium, which countries were freely importing American pork. The existence of this disease in Germany, therefore, he said, was due to native meats. All learned bodies, Minister Roche declared, have agreed that American meats were innocuous, and the admission of these meats into France would be the greatest boon to the working people of the country. It was more needful to beware of German meats entering France duty free. Furthermore, in spite of the prohibition on American meats, they actually entered France by indirect means.

Other members having spoken for and against the bill, the Government demanded its adoption, on the ground that the demand of the United States was legitimate, and that

France ought to comply with it in the interests of the trade of the two countries.

The motion was then adopted by a vote of 179 to 64, and the Senate proceeded to the discussion of the clauses of the measure.

I wonder whether the sovereigns, presidents, and ministers aforesaid know that the primary cause of the present differences was the quiet man from Filbert Street?

It is not my purpose here to discuss Dr. Leidy's contributions to a better understanding of human anatomy; in fact, it would make a *respectable* course of lectures to do so, and I can but indicate them.

He spent his time at the University in elucidating and illustrating them, whenever he could spare it from the preparation of his lectures in ordinary course. You will find them fully set forth in his admirable treatise on Human Anatomy, which *he* calls Elementary.

I was with him during many of these investigations, and many charming hours we have spent together in discussing them. I need but allude to the comparative anatomy of the liver, the development of the Purkinjean corpuscles in bone, and the development of the intermaxillary bone.

The structure of the *temporal* bone—here I

must stop for a moment to ask who would have thought of anything new in the description of that much-studied remarkable bone, and in the anatomy of the ear? And yet, see Dr. Leidy's wonderful display of them in specimens from his hand, now in the museum, and read carefully his accounts of them. There was a time, it seems to me, when he always had a temporal bone in one hand and a knife in the other. He aided me to select Politzer's fine case of ear specimens at the Centennial, which I purchased for the Mütter Museum, and when we obtained Hyrtl's preparations of the comparative anatomy of the ear, he was delighted. I must confess, however, that, for preparations of the human temporal bone, I greatly prefer those by Leidy himself, our own great master; for, without egotism, I profess to belong to the few who know what a good preparation is when they see it.

Dr. Leidy's description of the vocal membranes of the larynx is admirable, and that of the structure of the larynx and the attachment of its muscles is equally so. Thus, this many-sided man went on. To quote Dr. Chapman, "The variety, extent, and exactness of Dr. Leidy's knowledge of nature were unsurpassed, if equalled by any living naturalist. It was this familiarity with all natural objects, which invariably impressed those brought in personal contact with him. If some minute infusorian were casually mentioned in conversation, one would have supposed from his remarks that he had devoted his life to the study of the protozoa; an intestinal worm being the subject of discussion—from his description of its structure, origin, and mode of life, it would have been inferred that helminthology was his exclusive specialty. The opportunity of seeing him dissect an insect, mollusk, or vertebrate, would soon convince one that he was a most skilful anatomist. A fragment of rock, a plant, a shell submitted to him, called forth criticisms worthy of the professional mineralogist, botanist, or conchologist."

"Profound as was his knowledge of living plants and animals, it can be truly said that his acquaintance with the extinct forms of life was equally so. Indeed, it was his great familiarity with the existent types of vegetable and animal life, that so eminently qualified him to determine fossil forms."

When the Biological Department was established Dr. Leidy took a most active interest in it, and his work over here was much increased. He was a director in it and the Professor of Zoölogy. When it was fully organized, Dr. Jayne tells me, the doctor always occupied the chair and directed the proceedings. It was the hope of his life, Dr. Jayne also says, to bring the Academy of Natural Sciences and the Biological Department of the University closely together. That hope has not been realized as yet. Dr. Leidy's studies of the parasites and his work on the tertiary fossils of Florida were done in the Biological building. Dr. Dolley is now engaged in classifying and arranging the former. I had ample evidence the other day of the Biological being now able to stand alone, notwithstanding Dr. Leidy's disappointments about it and the Academy. The crowds of enthusiastic young men and some women (I am glad to say), each at their places at the tables, in the great working-room, and each with a microscope working out the lesson for the day, gave full proofs of prosperity.

Dr. Jayne's letter concludes: " His love for us was especially great, and he is missed every day. We expect to see his familiar form turn the corner of the street, and it is almost impossible to realize that another has his room and another gives his lectures."

At the Veterinary Department too, where the

doctor was Professor of Zoölogy, he was equally valued. No one had a more thorough knowledge of the structure and history of the domestic animals treated there than he. His knowledge of the horse from its origin in prehistoric days, gained from a profound study of the marvellous changes its fossil remains show that it had undergone before the peerless animal of to-day was produced, was incomparable. When I go over all of these matters I ask myself the question, "Did we work the doctor too hard?"

Were I to write to Swarthmore and to the Wagner Free Institute, I know that I would get the same kind of answers. A pretty Swarthmore story is told of Dr. Leidy, showing his dislike of inflicting unnecessary pain upon or taking the lives of animals he used for demonstration at his lectures. On a certain Saturday he caught some small creatures from the brooks and creeks near by for this purpose, and when he was through with them he laid them aside intending to return them to their native streams. He forgot to do this, and took the train for home. On Sunday morning he thought of them, and from their habits he knew they would not live till Monday unless furnished with water. Car communication with Swarthmore was slow on Sunday at that time. The morning train had gone, so the doctor walked all the way to Swarthmore and rescued his prisoners.[1]

[1] The Wagner Institute expressed their loss in the following minute :—

With feelings of deep sorrow we record the death of Dr. Joseph Leidy, who, for the past six years, has stood at the head of the science work of our Institute, as President of the Faculty, and Director of the Museum.

The death of this true and honest man, as gentle as he was strong, as humble as he was great, is to the whole civilized world, as it is to our own country, the loss of one of the most distinguished scientists of the day; while to Philadelphia, the city of his birth and his life-long home, it is the loss, not only of one of her greatest men, but as well of a true and faithful son, who loyally spent his whole life in her service, and who died, as he lived, in entire devotion to duty, wholly forgetful of himself, and mindful only of the welfare of others.

To the Wagner Free Institute of Science the loss occasioned by his death is beyond repair. The place he has left vacant cannot be filled. To him, more than to any other man, and to his good guidance more than to anything else, is due whatever has been accomplished by the Institute, since the death of its founder, in the organization and conduct of its work in the cause of science. It is impossible to express in words the debt of gratitude we owe to him; only by deeds can we give expression to it, by striving to so carry out the work which he has planned for us with such con-

How the doctor mourned the loss of his nucleus of a museum of natural history at Swarthmore when it was destroyed by fire a few years ago! He had grand but simple ideas of what a museum should be for the purposes of instruction, and many of them are now being carried out at the Biological. I could say much on this subject, but to enter upon it now would take up too much time for a discourse like that I am giving.

The only instance I ever knew of Dr. Leidy's departure from strict truth was, to a medical man's way of looking at it, a very amusing one. Some years ago he came to my house in quite an enthusiastic mood, and said, "Dr. Hunt, do you know that they are moving the bodies from a very old burying-ground down town to make way for improvements?" "Yes," I said. "Well," he went on, "two bodies turned into adipocere are there [this is an ammoniacal soap, and the bodies are commonly called *petrified bodies*]. They have been buried for nearly a hundred years, an old man and an old woman; nobody claims them, and they would be rare and instructive additions to our collections.

summate skill, that it may become a living memorial of his earnest labors, his broad intelligence, and his commanding knowledge.

Now, I think I can get them, and if you will take one for the Mütter Museum, I will take the other for the Wistar and Horner Museum." All right, I said, I shall be delighted. So down Leidy went, full of the idea of securing the prizes. When he spoke to the superintendent or caretaker of the ground, that gentleman put on airs, talked of violating graves, etc.; so the discomfited doctor was about going away quite chapfallen. Just then the caretaker touched him significantly on the elbow and said, "I tell you what I do; I give bodies up to the order of relatives!" The doctor immediately took the hint. He went home, hired a furniture wagon, and armed the driver with an order reading, "Please deliver to bearer the bodies of my grandfather and grandmother."

This brought the coveted prizes, and one is now in each of the museums, and the virtuous caretaker was amply compensated.

But they all do it. The great Hyrtl, of Vienna, he, whose work on Topographical Anatomy, I often say is my guide, philosopher, and friend, sent us over a catalogue some time ago of articles he wished us to purchase, and with great effrontery or great honesty, possibly that we should not doubt the verification, has these words affixed to the statement of the skull of some notable character, "Stolen by myself." I had occasion to write some lines to a lady, not long since, one who was much interested in a certain mortuary, and this is the way, in strict confidence, I tell her about this peculiar tendency in men medical.

I admit the fact, you will notice, and discuss the law—that is, the metaphysics of it, for I believe jurists have frequently declared there is no property in a dead body.

Now, I'll tell you a secret,
 That makes me grieve!
The fellows who post
 Will always thieve!

Though the corpus delicti is not quite clear,
 For 'tis plain a dead body can't say, "I am here,"
Or "It is I," "homo sum," "me too," or "Ego,"
For all are agreed he's above, or below.
So the posters don't worry as to tuum and meum,
But take the specimens for the museum.

I am in negotiation for some mummies now. The Egyptians hold on to them more tightly than they did to the Israelites. I have personally, and to my regret, found out that they will not give them up to the order of relatives.

(29)

What a delight it was to take an excursion with Dr. Leidy as one of the company! It made no difference in what direction; near home, as down in the Neck, where the nelumbium grew, or upon the Wissahickon Hills, or even about the city. I have heard him talk on cobblestones in a most instructive and delightful way. The stones of various buildings, the mineral and fungus deposits on the walls and pavements, the various layers of soil where cellars were being dug, the loams, clays, etc., he knew all about them. Sometimes we went to the mountains; sometimes to the coal regions; sometimes to the sea. In all he was equally at home. The botany, the geology, the paleontology, and mineralogy were at his finger-ends, and without any more assumption of superior knowledge than an infant.

How far he was from sordid thoughts! Like Agassiz, he had no time to make money!

On several occasions, when passing through places rich in mineral deposits, and full of the roar and bustle of industry, some one has said: "Why, Joe, you knew all about this years ago; you told me about it. Why did you not buy some of the land?" "Well, now, do you know I never thought of its having any money value; and should I have done so, I did not have the money!"

In September, 1881, we made a memorable excursion to Virginia. Its purpose was to dedicate one of the splendid columns and a stalactite to Dr. Leidy in the Cave of Luray, and to visit the Natural Bridge. The weather was fine, and the ladies and gentlemen of the party were much interested. One beautiful Sunday morning we went into the cave, and after inspecting its wonders we assembled in the chamber containing the objects to be dedicated. Miss Ally Leidy, the doctor's daughter, was furnished with a bottle filled with clear water from one of the pools in the cave. She was to break it at the appropriate moment on the column, in the same manner as at the launching and naming of a ship. The assembly was formed; the torches held aloft, lighted up the scene made brilliant by the reflections from the glittering stalactites and stalagmites. I was appointed orator, and my speech was short. I said :—

This column and that stalactite, in the Caverns of Luray, are dedicated to Dr. Joseph Leidy. From now on they will be known as the Leidy Column and the Leidy Stalactite. May they thus aid to perpetuate the name of one who, holding "communion with the visible forms of nature," has so learned to interpret her grand simplicity that to hear him is to understand.

Miss Ally did her part beautifully. The doctor made a few remarks, stating that he could not have been more highly honored than in having such grand objects named after him. (By the way, I should have stated that the purposes of the expedition were until this moment most successfully kept from the knowledge of the doctor.)

Quite different was the account of the ceremonies given outside by one of the young natives. We had it from one of the ladies of the party, who, having been in the cave before, did not go in now, but stayed outside upon the sunny porch. Her narrative amused Dr. Leidy hugely, both for itself as well as for the racial peculiarities which it showed.

About the entrance to the cave was a tribe of little darkies, mostly of pure blood. They blacked the boots and brushed the clothes of the visitors, for going into the cave is not a clean matter. Among them, however, was one very light mulatto, almost white, who went in with the party to see all that was to be seen, and he ran out ahead to join his fellows after the ceremonies were over. The lady said, "I know all about it; I've been listening to that little fellow who has been telling the others what he saw and heard. 'Great doin's in dar,' he said ; 'I runned out to tell you'uns bout it. Dey all got togeder in de big room, whar de big pillars is. De young misse hab a bottle full ob de cabe water. One genlm'n said suffin, anoder genlm'n said suffin, den dey all look solem like. Now, bust your bottle, says one ob de genlm'n, says he, and de misse bust de bottle, and name de pillar fur de genlm'n.' "

All were delighted with this description, and the ladies at once began to throw nickels and pennies to the boys who were down on the ground at the foot of the porch. The mulatto now began antics in every shape ; he threw wheels, and summersaults, and started everything prehensile in his body, even to his toes, and picked up by far most of the cash, showing that he was much sharper than his more deeply colored companions.

The excursion was extended to the Natural Bridge. Dr. Leidy said, I remember, that he had travelled much both at home and abroad, had seen many noted fine things, but he thought that the Natural Bridge and Niagara Falls were the two grandest *single* objects in nature that he had yet seen or heard of. The Falls are known the world over ; the Bridge is not nearly so well known, as it deserves to be.

Dr. Leidy has by no means been forgotten in dedications of grand natural objects to his memory.

Projecting into the solitudes of the icy northern seas from the east coast of Grinnell Land, the highest known land of the globe, in latitude 79° 45′ north, are two prominent capes bounding a bay between them. Drs. Elisha Kent Kane and Isaac I. Hayes discovered and named these in the famous expedition of 1854–5. They were faithful to their alma mater, for one was christened after their beloved friend and promising young naturalist, Cape Joseph Leidy, and the other after the learned and genial Professor of Chemistry in the Arts Department, Cape John Frazer. There was no need of bottles of water at these baptisms, for the breakers of those seas, except when stilled by ice, are eternally dashing on its shores. Thus you see the old University is remembered, through its professors and her alumni, even where the foot of man has rarely trod.

On the western slope of the Rockies, between 43° and 44° of N. latitude, and 110° and 111° of W. longitude, south of the Great National Park, in the State of Wyoming, stands Mount Leidy. It was named by Dr. F. V. Hayden, the distinguished explorer and geologist, in honor of his

treasured friend. We, of the Biological Club, recall with the greatest pleasure our meetings from
time to time with Dr. Hayden as a welcome guest.
Senator Penrose tells me that, with the exception
of the Tetons, Mount Leidy is the finest object in
the neighborhood, snow-capped and rising in soli-
tary grandeur above the plain. This past summer
he hunted over it with great satisfaction. By the
way, I must tell you that a recent graduate of the
University, and afterward a resident of the Pennsylvania Hospital, is now Governor of Wyoming,
Dr. Barber. Thus, Dr. Leidy, who has erected a
monument *for himself* more enduring than brass,
has had his name impressed by loving friends
deeply under the soil, as at Luray; high in the
Arctic regions, as by Kane and Hayes; and in the
wilds of Wyoming, as by Hayden. What his own
community at home will do to perpetuate his
memory remains to be seen.

Leidy was nothing if not Darwinian. He was
a firm believer in the doctrine of evolution, natural
selection, and the survival of the fittest. Dr. Chapman has, in his memoir, given a quotation from
Dr. Leidy before Darwin's Origin of Species ap-
peared, foreshadowing the same ideas.

Of course, the credit of fixing an idea through

experiment and observation remains, as it should do, with the fixer, but as in almost everything we find that the same ideas have dominated other minds. In my reading last winter I came across two passages from Addison which I copied for Dr. Leidy. He was greatly surprised, and put them carefully away, to use at some lecture this winter. Alas! we shall never hear of them through him.

Who would have thought of the great essayist and poet being a Darwinian? He says, in paper 120 of The Spectator, " My friend, Sir Roger, is very often merry with me upon my passing so much of my time among his poultry. He has caught me twice or thrice looking at a bird's nest, and several times sitting an hour or two together looking at a hen and chickens. He tells me he believes I am personally acquainted with every fowl about his house; calls such a particular cock my favorite; and frequently complains that his ducks and geese have more of my company than himself. I must confess I am infinitely delighted with those speculations of nature which are to be made in a country life; and as my reading has very much lain among books of natural history, I cannot forbear recollecting upon this occasion the several remarks which I have met with in authors and comparing them with what falls under my own observation, the arguments for Providence drawn from the natural history of animals being, in my opinion, demonstrative." Addison became more of an evolutionist, and it is in paper 519 that the true Darwinian thought is most felicitously given. It is no wonder that Johnson said, "Who wishes to attain an English style familiar, but not coarse, and elegant but not ostentatious, must give his days and nights to the volumes of Addison." Mark the last passage of the following quotation; Dr. Leidy enjoyed it much : " There are some living creatures which are raised just above dead matter. To mention only that species of shell-fish which are formed in the fashion of a cone, that grow to the surface of several rocks, and immediately die upon being severed from the place upon which they grow. There are many other creatures but one remove from these which have no other sense besides that of feeling and taste, others have still an additional one of hearing ; others of smell and others of sight.

"It is wonderful to observe by what a gradual progress the world of life advances through a *prodigious variety* of species before a creature is formed that is complete in all its senses ; and even among these there is such a different degree of perfection in the sense which one animal enjoys beyond what appears in another that, though the sense in different animals be distinguished by the same common denomination, it seems almost of a different nature. If after this we look into the several inward perfections of cunning and sagacity, or what we generally call instinct, we find them rising after the same manner *imperceptibly* one above another, according to the species in which they are implanted. *This progress in nature is so very gradual that the most perfect of an inferior species comes very near to the most imperfect of that which is immediately above it."* How like Darwin in the first extract, making observations at home among homely animals! How very like him in the last, making, to my mind, deductions fully in accord with the doctrine of evolution !

Now Addison was born in 1672 and died in 1719. Lamarck, the great French naturalist, who was closely on the track of Darwin, was born in 1744 and died in 1829 ; and Darwin himself was born in 1809 and died in 1882. So the poet and man of letters preceded the others for many years in the same line of thought.

Any thing from the smallest to the greatest

that bore upon the theory of evolution interested Dr. Leidy extremely. This walking-stick [showing stick] greatly awakened his interest. It was brought from abroad by a friend of mine and given to me on the condition that it must be first shown to Dr. Leidy, and if he could not tell what it was I would be told. I saw that it was herbaceous and said so. Dr. Leidy was puzzled for once, and got no further in a diagnosis, whereupon I wrote to my friend, and he answered, telling what the cane is. It is a strip or shoot of the wild cabbage. The cabbages (genus Brassica) are originally sea plants. Among other places near the sea this wild form grows upon the Channel Islands, and sometimes at certain stages it sends up these shoots. Those fit for walking-sticks are selected by the natives and sold as curiosities. So I learnedly write to Dr. Leidy an extract from Knight's Encyclopædia (the writer must have been a good Darwinian): "This glaucous plant has a somewhat woody stem, having but slender likeness to its cultivated progeny; and it is difficult to conceive by what original discoverer the species was brought under the influence of domestication so as to have been prepared for the numerous changes and improvements it had to undergo before the races of cabbages, savoys, borecoles, cauliflowers, and broccolis could have been produced." I received this answer :—

DEAR DR. HUNT : I am not surprised to hear the cane is from the "wild cabbage," which I had never seen, nor would I have guessed its origin. A number of cultivated plants which are tender and succulent are woody in the wild condition, instance the root of the carrot, etc. Do not the many varieties of cabbage you mention favor the evolution theory?

Yours respectfully,
JOSEPH LEIDY.

The doctor's singleness of purpose in his devotion to science, no matter what might be the associations, is illustrated in the following incident for which the Rev. Mr. Burk, our secretary, is responsible. Burk and Leidy met in a street car. They sat down together and Leidy began at once : "I have wanted to see you, to know if you still keep your little church in the country." Burk answered solemnly, "Yes, I am still able to retain it." Burk was surprised, for he thought that Leidy had experienced a change and was about opening a conversation on the soul's state of the average Jerseyman. Now, it so happens, that Mr.

Burk's church and residence are in a neighborhood where there are marl pits, and in those having water in them, a large thin-shelled mussel, or unio, grows which is very interesting, as to its origin and mode of development in that place. So this was the Jerseyman that Dr. Leidy was after, and, with a pause showing much relief, he said, "I am very glad, indeed, to hear that you still have the church—very glad. You will keep your eye on that *unio fragilis*, I hope."

How fond Dr. Leidy was of gems! He knew as much or more about them than the most finished jewellers. He had quite a valuable collection of them which he sold some time before his death. His liking for them came not only from their intrinsic beauty, but because they were *natural* objects, and for all such objects we have seen that his appetite was omnivorous.

Various stories are told of ladies driving to the doctor's house in order to get his judgment upon diamonds, rubies, sapphires, and other precious stones before purchasing, and he always gave the information unerringly and was amused at the fees tendered by the callers who innocently thought it was his business.

A gentleman told me that a few days after the

doctor's death he was in a shop kept by a lapidary quite learned in his calling. A stranger to my friend came in, and the lapidary asked him if he knew what a certain fine stone was. The stranger answered he did not, and the lapidary said, " I also don't know. Ah ! there was only one man who could have told you what it is, but he is dead."

Dr. Leidy was a giant in intellect, a saint in disposition. I often marvel at what the world calls *greatness*. Who understands the mystery of why he who constructs a gun, or invents a shell which will kill, crush, and mangle more at a shot, than the gun that was in use the year before, is enriched, ennobled, and glorified, and made the associate of princes, whilst the practical discoverers of anæsthesia died in poverty and neglect? Who of you would not rather have his name associated in the humblest way with the introducers of that great boon to humanity, than to have all the wealth won from guns, and shot, and shell? It is truly a mystery ! It seems to be more praiseworthy to destroy than to save, " *Aus Finsterniss zum Licht, durch Blut,*" is the grim legend of the black, white, and red Prussian flag—out of darkness into light, through blood !—and this seems to be an epitome of the history of the world's progress. Leidy rightly called it a process of evolution. The thoroughly subdued races and tribes, "the dead nations, never rise again;" *they make the paleontology of peoples!* The conqueror moves on a higher plane, and adds *in time* something to the general good; surely it is a mystery! Is war then the natural state of man? We who are old enough to have participated in it, to a greater or less degree, and to have heard and seen its "loud lament and dismal miserere," want no more of it, but we fondly look forward to a realization, however remote, of what Love says to Death in the fine sonnet of Tennyson, which, I know from conversations, expresses the hopes and views of Dr. Leidy :—

> "This hour is thine :
> Thou art the shadow of life, and as the tree
> Stands in the sun and shadows all beneath,
> So in the light of great eternity,
> Life eminent creates the shade of death ;
> The shadow passeth, when the tree shall fall,
> But *I* shall reign forever over all."

And thus our Leidy passed through life, with peace and love in his heart, leaving to us who honored him for his intellect, and loved him for the gentleness that made him great, the right to laud him as a beacon light of science !

In Memoriam.

DR. JOSEPH LEIDY.

B. Sept. 9, 1823.   D. April 30, 1891.

PERSONAL HISTORY.

BY

WILLIAM HUNT, M.D.

READ AT THE ACADEMY OF NATURAL SCIENCES,
MAY 12, 1891.

LOGAN SQUARE, May 7, 1891.

A MEETING in commemoration of JOSEPH LEIDY, M.D., LL.D., the late President of the Society, will be held in the Hall of the Academy, Tuesday, the 12th inst., at 8 P.M. Addresses will be made as follows :—

WILLIAM HUNT, M.D., " Personal History."

HARRISON ALLEN, M.D., "Work in Vertebrate Anatomy."

HENRY C. CHAPMAN, M.D., "Work in Invertebrate Anatomy."

PROF. ANGELO HEILPRIN, "Work in Paleontology and Geology."

JOSEPH WILLCOX, " Work in Mineralogy."

JAMES DARRACH, M.D., " Work in Botany."

EDWARD J. NOLAN, M.D., " Personal Character and Services to the Academy."

It is expected that further remarks will be made by other members.

EDWARD J. NOLAN,
Recording Secretary.

The meeting was large, and attended both by men and women. It was a most remarkable occasion. The originals of the addresses, which were limited to fifteen or twenty minutes each, are preserved in the archives of the Academy.

Dr. HENRY C. CHAPMAN has been appointed to write a full memoir of this great student of nature, which will be published in the *Proceedings* of the Academy.

W. H.

(48)

In Memoriam.

DR. JOSEPH LEIDY.

By WILLIAM HUNT, M.D.

IT is fitting that we imagine the beloved subject of our discourses this evening to be with us in spirit, as he doubtless is in influence, and to let him introduce himself, as I heard him do in Association Hall some years ago, where he was about to give a popular lecture. I was unexpectedly called upon to introduce him: "What!" said I. "Who is to introduce the introducer? Here's a man more widely known to the city and to the world than any of us!" Dr. Leidy, hearing the conversation, said: "Oh! Dr. Hunt, keep your seat; I don't wish to be introduced; I'll introduce myself." And, stepping to the rostrum, he spoke in this way:

"My name is Joseph Leidy, doctor of medicine. I was born in this city on the 9th of September, 1823, and I have lived here ever since. My father was Philip Leidy, the hatter, on Third Street, above Vine. My mother was Catharine Mellick, but she died a few months after my birth. My father married her sister, Christina Mellick, and she was the mother I have known, who was all in all to me, the one to whom I owe all that I am. At an early age I took great delight in natural history, and in noticing all natural objects. I have reason to think that I know a little of natural history, and a little of that little I propose to teach you to-night."

This, of course, brought down the house. I never heard such a good introduction; but I little thought that the incident would serve me to introduce him on this mournful occasion.

When a boy, so great was his love for the country that it was difficult to keep him at school. He took every opportunity for a run or walk in the fields, and is said to have left school without permission for this purpose. His mother employed a colored attendant to look after him, for off he would go if he could, and he took the chances of punishment or reproof at home. When ten years old he sketched pictures of natural objects. A book of sketches of shells, made when he was twelve, is in the possession of his nephew, Dr. Joseph Leidy, Jr.

Dr. Leidy's mother was intelligent, ambitious, and literary. She regarded a good education as the best heritage for her children. She wished her sons to study the professions. I saw her once, and I remember her as a noble-looking woman.

It is well that she was the ruling spirit, for the father, I am told, had rather a contempt for professional men, and wished his sons to learn trades. Noticing Joseph's facility with the pencil, he wished him to be an artist. The mother's wishes, however, prevailed ; but the father was not wholly convinced of the correctness of her judgment until years after.

She had several sons, and when the war came she decided that all should go. Even the doctor took his·part, and became an acting surgeon of the U. S. Army. He was assigned to hospital duty, and was chiefly occupied in the study and preparation of pathological specimens. The Army Medical Museum at Washington contains some of these, which are fully described in its records.

Dr. Leidy began the study of medicine in 1840, and graduated at the University of Pennsylvania in 1844. His graduating thesis showed the bent of his mind. It was upon the "Comparative Anatomy of the Eye of Vertebrated Animals." He became Demonstrator of Anatomy in the Franklin Medical College, to which new institution he was no doubt attracted by the genius and reputation of Dr. Paul B. Goddard, who was his preceptor. He gave lectures on Microscopic Anatomy. His advance now was rapid, for, in 1852, when it was necessary at the University to appoint an assistant for Dr. Horner, whose health was failing, Dr. Leidy was chosen for the place. Dr. Horner died soon after; and in 1853 Dr. Leidy was elected Professor of Anatomy in the University of Pennsylvania, when he was in the thirtieth year of his age. He was holding this position at the time of his death, and, therefore, held it for thirty-eight years. In 1854 he appointed me Demonstrator of Anatomy in the University, and thus, by this choice, I was for ten years, during the sessions at least, necessarily brought into daily intercourse with him, which intercourse ripened into loving and lasting companionship. During all this association I never had an unpleasant word with him; and yet he could be indignant, but his indignations were with ideas and not with persons.

This angelic amiability never for a moment brought disrespect; there was a dignity with it that mastered all. I cannot recall a single attempt to play a student's trick upon him; and I never saw upon the walls or in the class-rooms any ridicule of him, either in doggerel or in drawing. The stories told of him were all beauties, or marvels at his wondrous learning, or at what he could do with his eyes, his hands, and his microscope.

Dr. Leidy taught pure anatomy; others of us applied the knowledge he gave. This was all he said he would do, or engage to do. I mention this for you who are not familiar with such matters. Think of this! Could a man enjoy higher praise than to know that for thirty-eight years he filled without objection a practical chair in an essentially practical school for science, and science alone? In all that time, no jealous aspirant even whispered, "This chair must be practically filled." The lustre he threw upon the University dimmed or quenched all jealousies by its brightness. Professors, students, and all, behold how they loved him!

The personal history of Dr. Leidy is all that has been assigned me to talk about for these few minutes; and, therefore, I leave to others the task of speaking of his University scientific career.

Such a pronounced character could not but have its peculiarities. He was emotional to a degree. Music and the gentler sentiments stirred him deeply. If I were talking of a dear friend of his in his presence, as I am now talking of him, his eyes would be brimful of tears at the thoughts of that friend. Yet he professed to dislike poetry, and could not understand how we enjoyed the "rhyming stuff." At the Biological Club, a social organization of which he was President, he would sit at table either amused or absent-minded or lost in thought whilst poetical recitations were being given. Whilst, then, he did not read poetry in general, some of it touched him deeply. Whittier's poem, "The Prayer of Agassiz," a "wordless prayer" upon the opening of the Anderson School of Natural History, at Penikese, stirred him and pleased him wonderfully; over and over he read it, and spoke of it again and again. He greatly admired the "Chambered Nautilus" of Holmes. I recommended him to read the "Thanatopsis," which he had never done, and that grand poem also, as Friends say, "met the witness within." The motion of the hidden fire was there, and, I have no doubt, at times trembled in his breast. I am reminded, through speaking of the " wordless prayer," how Leidy's connection with Swarthmore brought him in contact with Friends, and he frequently spoke in admiration of the simplicity of their ways and their methods of worship.

To any analyzer of mind, it would be rather absurd to say that this lover of flowers and fields and woods and brooks, this man who gloated over jewels and named some of his pretty polyps after beautiful women, had no poetry in his soul.

The imagination, in fact, properly directed, is a handmaid of science. I have elsewhere said that the great Goethe, one of the early leaders of scientific thought, mixed science and poetry in the same crucible, and, subjecting it to the heat of his imagination, poured out immortal ingots.

Leidy admitted this, but insisted on the proper direction towards Nature's facts, and not towards unreasoning or grotesque fancies. The conventional angel, for example, being a *six-limbed mammal*, was an impossibility for him, and he marvelled how it had been perpetuated from time immemorial by artists, sculptors, and the Church.

Dr. Leidy wrecked more mare's-nests than any man I ever heard of. It would take a volume to record the wonderful discoveries and the more wonderful specimens that were reported or brought to him almost daily, either personally or by mail. Petrified eggs, and tumors of orange pulp, and living worms of the same material were common incidents. New old animals, unknown minerals, mostly artificial, invaluable jewels, mostly of no value at all, and cures for all evils were presented for his opinion, his inspection, his name and patronage.

The quick and quiet way with which he would expose these wonders and treasures was a sight to see. And yet he did it with a grace and ease that had no pretension about it, so that the disappointed visitor went away under no provocation, but simply a sadder and a wiser man.

When anything really new was brought for his opinion he was much interested and most gracious.

It was by no means always the ignorant who were confounded. Many of us have heard him tell with glee of the incident (I think at Charleston, S. C.) where he was entertained at dinner by eminent scientific men. One of the luxuries was the tail of a drumfish, and even it had its tidbit, or choice part with the epicures, in the shape of a peculiar gelatinous mass. A part of this was helped with high praise to Dr. Leidy. He ate it, but his suspicions were aroused. He confirmed the truth of them fully by going to market next morning and examining a drumfish's tail. He found that the choice part was a huge parasite which, I think, he afterwards described. As the piece was well cooked, he said the eating of it did no harm.

On the other hand, when caught himself (which rarely happened), he behaved beautifully. I remember walking with him along the grassy path by the seaside, at Bar Harbor, one summer day. We were on our way to visit a Philadelphia lady who was herself an amateur botanist, and particularly well acquainted with the region about us. Suddenly, Dr. Leidy said, raising his hands, " Dear me ! There is a plant which Gray says only grows high on the mountains, and here it is by the sea." He gathered a portion of it with great care and put it in his pocket. When he got to the house he spoke of his find, and showed Mrs. —— the specimen. " Why, doctor," she said, " that is *Empetrum*." The doctor looked carefully at it and said, " Why, so it is ; I thought it was *Loiseleuria*," and he laughed heartily, receiving the correction as though it had come from Gray himself.

Dr. Leidy loved dearly the company of his friends, in a social way. Besides presiding at the Biological Club, he was a Director of the old Contributionship on Fourth Street, and enjoyed the monthly meetings very much.

His place at table was always a point of interest, and many regarded it as a privilege to sit near him, so attractive was his instructive conversation, and so frequent were the appeals made to him from all sides for information. The late lamented Sydney Biddle, the youngest member of our Club, Dr. Leidy told me, with much feeling, made the request at my house that at the next meeting he might have the privilege of sitting by him. Both now are gone!

In person Dr. Leidy was a blonde, of medium height and stout frame. He wore a full beard, and had fine, silken, flowing hair. His forehead was beautiful, but by no means pronounced. His almost straight brows overhung rather deeply set, very thoughtful, and somewhat pensive blue eyes. His nose was of the aquiline order and finely cut. His mouth, medium in size, with flexible, well-formed lips backed by fine teeth, had great range of expression.

In early manhood Dr. Leidy's face bore a

striking likeness to the familiar pictures of the Saviour, and several pretty stories are told of confiding little children coming unto him attracted by the resemblance. One of these I have direct. The doctor was being entertained one Sunday in the country by a former member of this Academy, now dead. The company started out for a walk. A little daughter of the host joined them and walked with her father; suddenly she broke away and ran over the grass in chase of a butterfly. After much exertion she caught it, brought it back to the company, and whispered in her father's ear that it was for Jesus Christ, and timidly gave it to the doctor.

In reviewing what I have written, I see that it would be natural for some one to say, " You have described a perfect man ! Had he no faults ?" As there is but *One* all-perfect, of course he had faults, but I do not know them.

No one disbelieves the sentimental " *De mortuis nil*" more than I do. I have declaimed against it, for, if it prevailed, history and biography would be useless. In this case, however, I can simply repeat, after much thought, " I find no fault in this man."

The end was approaching. Dr. Leidy worked

through the past session of the University feeling the mental and physical effects of his labors more and more. Frequently he sat down during half of his lecture. The examinations came on, and they exhausted him greatly. He said, "The old machine is breaking up."

About two weeks before he died he attended the funeral of Aubrey H. Smith, also one of the honored members of this Academy. I occupied a seat during that "hour's communion with the dead," which gave me a full view of the doctor, who sat at one end of a sofa near the coffin, his face buried in his hands. He was evidently in deep thought. He left the house and turned up Pine Street alone, much bowed down, and possibly contemplating his own near call.

On the Thursday following he took to his bed. On Saturday, whilst he was still sensible, his daughter showed him a sprig of Mayflower. "What beautiful *Epigea!*" he said; "do you remember what the name means?" He shortly after lapsed into unconsciousness, which became deeper and deeper until he died.

In truth, then, at the close, he laid down in green pastures.

www.ingramcontent.com/pod-product-compliance
Lightning Source LLC
Chambersburg PA
CBHW031320280626
47169CB00019B/2563